EVERYTHING COMES NEXT

NAOMI SHIHAB NYE

EVERYTHING COMES NEXT

Collected & New Poems

ILLUSTRATIONS BY Rafael López

WITH AN INTRODUCTION BY Edward Hirsch

Greenwillow Books
An Imprint of HarperCollins*Publishers*

Everything Comes Next: Collected and New Poems
Copyright © 1994, 1995, 1998, 2000, 2001, 2002, 2004,
2005, 2008, 2011, 2018, 2019, 2020 by Naomi Shihab Nye
Introduction by Edward Hirsch
Interior illustrations by Rafael López

The permissions acknowledged on page 235
are a continuation of this copyright page.

The text of this book is set in 11-point Warnock Pro.
Book design by Paul Zakris

Library of Congress Cataloging-in-Publication Data

Names: Nye, Naomi Shihab, author.
Title: Everything comes next : collected and new poems /
by Naomi Shihab Nye.
Description: First edition. | New York, NY :
Greenwillow Books, an Imprint of HarperCollinsPublishers, [2020] |
Includes index. | Audience: Ages 8-12 | Audience: Grades 4-6 |
Summary: "Everything Comes Next contains Naomi Shihab Nye's most beloved poems, including "Famous," "A Valentine for Ernest Mann," "Kindness," and "Gate A-4," as well as new, unpublished poems. It is an introduction to the poet's work for new readers, as well as a comprehensive edition for classrooms"—Provided by publisher.
Identifiers: LCCN 2020029358 | ISBN 9780063013452 (hardback) |
ISBN 9780063013476 (ebook)
Subjects: LCGFT: Poetry.
Classification: LCC PS3564.Y44 E94 2020 | DDC 811/.54—dc23
LC record available at https://lccn.loc.gov/2020029358

20 21 22 23 24 PC/LSCH 10 9 8 7 6 5 4 3 2 1
First Edition

GREENWILLOW BOOKS

To all readers and writers of poems everywhere

Be brave

Little things

still matter most

Contents

THE HOLY LAND THAT ISN'T

PEOPLE ARE THE ONLY HOLY LAND

"May we regard the reading life of the young as the most vital homeland protection strategy going—for our home is this planet and our family the wide-flung tribes who shelter therein."

—Gregory Maguire, from a speech at
"The World Is All Grown Strange" (CLNE Institute)

Introduction

As a poet, Naomi Shihab Nye brings a fresh perspective to the world. Her poems are neighborly and hard-won, playful and instructive, canny and wise. She pays close attention and notices things that might otherwise be overlooked—sometimes by gazing at them directly, sometimes by catching them from the corner of her eye. For example, she answers a typical question about how she became a writer with a little poem that takes aim at those two clichéd figures from one of our first children's books, those dumbbells Dick and Jane: "Possibly I began writing as a refuge from our insulting first grade textbook. *Come, Jane, come. Look, Dick, look.* Were there ever duller people in the world? You had to tell them to look at things? Why weren't they looking at things to begin with?" We all start out noticing things, Nye reminds us, we just need to value what we see. That's why nothing is too small or out-of-the-way for her to observe. Her poems are utterly clear but secretly cunning, and she is like William Blake, the great English poet of innocence as well as experience, who knew it was possible "To see a World in a Grain of Sand."

Children are everywhere in Nye's work. She treats childhood

not just as a time of life but also as a sacred place, almost a country of its own. That's why she names the first section of this book "The Holy Land of Childhood." She is very loyal to that country, which knows no boundaries, and states outright that "the one flag we all share is the beautiful flag of childhood." It is a colorful flag and waves over all our heads, like a banner.

Sometimes Nye recalls her own childhood, other times she observes the childhoods of others. She writes as a parent, a visiting poet, a teacher dropped into someone else's classroom. She is especially alert to the oddball and insightful things that kids say, like "I never want to minus you" and "It's hard to be a person" and "I do and don't love you—/ isn't that happiness?" Nye notes these bold mottoes not because they are "cute" but because they express unexpected feelings, strange truths.

Nye frequently takes the child's point of view in her poems— the French writer Jean Cocteau quipped that "there are poets and grown-ups"—and writes with an innate feeling that children are often lonely and afraid. They feel unprotected, manipulated by adults in ways they don't like or even understand. Nye tries to address these feelings of isolation and loneliness. She believes that poems connect people, libraries open up our lives, and no one is alone who has a beloved book for company. You have a trusted companion in a book. Poetry is expressive and useful because it helps us to understand ourselves better. It also enables us to understand other people, especially people who are different than we are. The poet and the reader may not know each other personally, but they share an intimacy that is irreplaceable. Sometimes, when you read a poem, you feel as if the poet is speaking directly to you, maybe even that the poem was made particularly for you. In this way, Nye sees the task of the poet as both humble and hopeful. Hence the close of one of her most famous poems, "Famous": "I want to be famous in the way a pulley is famous, / or a buttonhole, / not because it did anything spectacular, / but because it never forgot what it could do."

Naomi Shihab Nye is a Palestinian American poet, and the second section of this book is called "The Holy Land That Isn't." This section begins with a set of touching poems about her father, Aziz Shihab, whose family lost their home in Jerusalem. After that, they moved to a West Bank village in 1948. He emigrated to the United States and became a distinguished Arab American journalist in Texas. Nye takes to heart her father's sadness and longing for a lost homeland, his proud memories, his enduring hopefulness. She is indignant about what has happened not just to him but to his entire family, one side of her heritage, and this gives her a personal stake in seeking justice for generations of refugees, displaced and occupied people. War isn't a game, it has deep human consequences. But she doesn't get on soapboxes and give lectures, she doesn't write about the Israeli-Palestinian conflict from a grand geopolitical perspective but from a homespun, local point of view, an intimate human perspective. She is down-to-earth and says, "You don't think what a little plot of land means / till someone takes it and you can't go back." The suffering of other people is one of the touchstones of her work. She keeps people firmly in view whenever she is writing about politics—or anything else. She is stubborn and determined to move forward, to resist hatred and vengefulness, which is how she finds the title for this book: "There's a place in this brain / where hate won't grow. / I touch its riddle: wind, and seeds. / Something pokes us as we sleep. / It's late but everything comes next."

It makes sense for Nye to title the third section of this book "People Are the Only Holy Land," but it's a radical thing to say. We typically think of the Holy Land as an actual place, an ancient country, a physical region with spiritual significance, but Nye redefines it to say that the historical place or places, the physical patches of land, don't matter nearly as much as the people themselves—people who live everywhere. In other words, she saves her patriotism not for countries but for people themselves, who have childhoods and families, very specific histories. It is human beings, life itself, that she considers sacred. Indeed, her unwavering focus on people and their stories, their inner lives, is one of the main features of her work. That's why she makes so much of a man crossing the street in the rain with his son on his shoulder. "We're not going to be able / to live in this world / if we're not willing to do what he's doing / with one another."

Naomi Shihab Nye is an open-hearted singer who believes in poetry's verbal power to bring us together and care for each other, to recognize our sorrows and our sufferings, to heal our wounds and treasure our solitudes. She is one of our necessary poets of hopefulness.

—Edward Hirsch

Poetry

The library shelves opened their arms. In the library everyone was rich. I stacked my bounty, counting books, arranging their spines. Bindings of new books smelled delicious.

On television, the poet Carl Sandburg strummed his guitar, his voice a honey-sweet dream of rolling, rollicking words. Cats and fog and syllables on the wind. His white hair looked lit up from inside, like a lightbulb. I read every morning, every night. If you knew how to read, you could never be lonely.

If you knew how to read, it made sense that you might, one night in a tall Chicago hotel, ask for a large piece of pale construction paper—not the easiest thing to come by in a hotel—and write down something you felt that day when you saw the streets that were also bridges lifting up for boats to pass under. When you tipped your head back to gaze at the giant towers in which a thousand people worked who had never even *thought* of your name. It was worth saying.

You could take it to school and give it to your first-grade teacher, who didn't like you. Pretend it was a present. She would hang it on the bulletin board in the hall and weeks later, far from that trip, a girl in school who was bigger than you would pause to say, "Did you write that poem?"

"Ho! Yes, I almost forgot."

She smiled. "I read it—and I know what you mean," skipping off to join her friends at the monkey bars.

She knew what I *meant*. That was something. That was a wing to fly on all the way home, or for the rest of a life.

—Naomi Shihab Nye

THE HOLY LAND
OF CHILDHOOD

Come with Me

To the quiet minute

Between two noisy minutes

It's always waiting ready to welcome us

Tucked under the wing of the day

I'll be there

Where will you be?

Courage

A word must travel through

a tongue and teeth and wide air

to get there.

A word has tough skin.

To be let in,

a word must slide and sneak

and spin into the tunnel of the ear.

What's to fear?

Everything.

But a word

is brave.

Messages from Everywhere

light up our backyard.

A bird that flew five thousand miles

is trilling six bright notes.

This bird flew over mountains and valleys

and tiny dolls and pencils

of children I will never see.

Because this bird is singing to me,

I belong to the wide wind,

the people far away who share

the air and the clouds.

Together we are looking up

into all we do not own

and we are listening.

Please Describe How You Became a Writer

Possibly I began writing as a refuge from our insulting first grade textbook. *Come, Jane, come. Look, Dick, look.* Were there ever duller people in the world? You had to tell them to look at things? Why weren't they looking to begin with?

How to Paint a Donkey

She said the head
was too large

the hooves
too small

You could clean your paintbrush
but you couldn't get rid of that voice

While they watched
you crumpled him

let his blue body
stain your hands

You cried
when he hit the can

She smiled
You could try again

Maybe this is what I unfold

in the dark

deciding

for the rest of my life

That donkey

was just the right size

Supple Cord

My brother, in his small white bed,

held one end.

I tugged the other

to signal I was still awake.

We could have spoken,

could have sung

to one another,

we were in the same room

for five years,

but the soft cord

with its little frayed ends

connected us

in the dark,

gave comfort

even if we had been bickering

all day.

When he fell asleep first

and his end of the cord

dropped to the floor,

I missed him terribly,

though I could hear his steady breath

and we had such long and separate lives

ahead.

Yellow Glove

What can a yellow glove mean in a world of cars and governments?

I was small, like everyone. Life was a string of precautions: Don't kiss the squirrel before you bury him, suck candy, pop balloons, drop watermelons, watch TV. When the new gloves appeared one Christmas, I heard it trailing me: Don't lose the yellow gloves.

I was small, there was too much to remember. One day, waving at a stream—the ice had cracked, winter chipping down, soon we would sail boats and roll into ditches—I let a glove go. Into the stream, sucked under the street. Since when did streets have mouths? I walked home on a desperate road. Gloves cost money. We didn't have much. I would tell no one. I would wear the yellow glove that was left and keep the other hand in a pocket. I knew my mother's eyes had tears they had not cried yet. I didn't want to be the one to make them flow. It was the prayer I spoke secretly, folding socks, lining up donkeys in windowsills, *to be good,* a promise made to the roaches who scouted my closet at night, *if you don't get in my bed, I will be good.* And they listened. I had a lot to fulfill.

The months rolled down like towels out of a machine. I sang and drew and fattened the cat. *Don't scream, don't lie, don't cheat, don't fight*—you could hear it anywhere. A pebble could show you how to be smooth, tell the truth. A field could show how to sleep without walls. A stream could remember how to drift and change—next June I was stirring the stream like a soup, telling my brother dinner would be ready if he'd only hurry up with the bread, when I saw it. The yellow glove draped on a twig. A muddy survivor. A quiet flag.

Where had it been in the three gone months? I could wash it, fold it in my winter drawer with its sister, no one in that world would ever know. There were miracles on Harvey Street. Children walked home in yellow light. Trees were reborn and gloves traveled far, but returned. A thousand miles later, what can a yellow glove mean in a world of bankbooks and stereos?

Part of the difference between floating and going down.

Always Bring a Pencil

There will not be a test.
It does not have to be
a Number 2 pencil.

But there will be certain things—
the quiet flush of waves,
ripe scent of fish,
smooth ripple of the wind's second name—
that prefer to be written about
in pencil.

It gives them more room
to move around.

The Way They Talk about Art

You'd think it was a giant

with a vague face

a face you recognize

but can't really describe

everyone has seen it

at one time or another

vanishing into the hills

mysterious Bigfoot

leaving footprints

so infatuating

they spend millions of dollars

to lure him out

while all the art I've ever known

is very small

lives in miniature caves in the hillside

and comes out for crumbs

Sometimes I pretend

I'm not me,
I only work for me.

This feels like
a secret motor
chirring inside my mind.

I think, *She will be so glad*
when she sees the homework
neatly written.

She will be relieved
someone sharpened pencils,
folded clothes.

Making a Fist

For the first time, on the road north of Tampico,

I felt the life sliding out of me,

drum in the desert, harder and harder to hear.

I was seven, I lay in the car

watching palm trees swirl a sickening pattern past the glass.

My stomach was a melon split wide inside my skin.

"How do you know if you are going to die?"

I begged my mother.

We had been traveling for days.

With strange confidence she answered,

"When you can no longer make a fist."

Years later I smile to think of that journey,

the borders we must cross separately,

stamped with our unanswerable woes.

I who did not die, who am still living,

still lying in the backseat behind all my questions,

clenching and opening one small hand.

Sifter

When our English teacher gave

our first writing invitation of the year,

Become a kitchen implement

in 2 descriptive paragraphs, I did not think

butcher knife or frying pan,

I thought immediately

of soft flour showering through the little holes

of the sifter and the sifter's pleasing circular

swishing sound, and wrote it down.

Rhoda became a teaspoon,

Roberto a funnel,

Jim a muffin tin,

and Forrest a soup pot.

We read our paragraphs out loud.

Abby was a blender. Everyone laughed

and acted giddy but the more we thought about it,

we were all everything in the whole kitchen,

drawers and drainers, singing teapot and grapefruit spoon

with serrated edges, we were all

the empty cup, the tray.

This, said our teacher, *is the beauty of metaphor.*

It opens doors.

What I could not know then

was how being a sifter

would help me all year long.

When bad days came,

I would close my eyes and feel them passing

through the tiny holes.

When good days came,

I would try to contain them gently

the way flour remains

in the sifter until you turn the handle.

Time, time. I was a sweet sifter in time

and no one ever knew.

The House Made of Rain

Our voices poured out through
a hole in the floor.
Some days the woman with a bucket
came swaggering up the block
singing our names, the song that goes
old old very old
and we rode in her wake, echoing
the thrum of her lowest note.

At night the houses would tilt
like small boats on the Mississippi
and we fell away from one another
deep deep very deep
and I dreamed I held a hand
after the person who owned it was dead.

Already I felt the press of currents,
the taunt of a word like *blend.*
Our school herded us to the confluence of rivers,

I expected to see purple pouring into blue,

but just a subtle gray mingling.

I folded my arms.

They should see my house, I thought.

They should stand on the porch one afternoon

and hear what goes on.

In my house tears welled up from underground pools,

shadowy streams we rode from room to room,

paddling. Sometimes my brother pulled me out

though he had been premature and took a long time

to grow huge. A girl in my class said she had never

seen her parents sad. I wanted to drown in her life.

A floor furnace we had to leap over

or burn our feet, a barrel where we lit

what we wanted to lose, a red stove that has followed me

like a dog. That house still floats among houses

where neighbors used crutches, measured hems.

Thrum thrum from the bottom of the lung

The tornado that razored away whole blocks

might be coming back.

I rode my rocking horse hard as I could

to escape, and threw up.

Mama stroked my back. I told you to slow down, she said.

We were huddled in the hall. I told you, take it easy.

Next time, she said, could you please listen?

Living with Mistakes

They won't wear boots.
They march ahead of us
into our rooms, dripping.

Give them a chair.
Where they sit,
the fabric will be wet
for days.
We have to talk about
everything else
in their presence.

Boy and Mom at the Nutcracker Ballet

There's no talking in this movie.

> It's not a movie! Just watch the dancers.
> They tell the story through their dancing.

Why is the nutcracker mean?

> I think because the little boy broke him.

Did the little boy mean to?

> Probably not.

Why did the nutcracker stab his sword through the mouse
king? I liked the mouse king.

> So did I. I don't know. I wish that part wasn't in it.

You can see that girl's underpants.

> It's not underpants. It's a costume called a "tutu."

That's the same word as "grandma" in Hawaiian!

Are those really gems on their costumes?

Do they get to keep them?

Is that really snow coming down?

No, it can't be, it would melt and their feet get wet.

I think it's white paper.

Aren't they beautiful?

They are very beautiful. But what do the dancers do
when we can't see them, when they're off the stage
and they're not dancing?

Do you have any more pistachios in your purse?

So There

Because I would not let one four-year-old son

eat frosted mini-wheat cereal

fifteen minutes before supper

he wrote a giant note

and held it up

LOVE HAS FAILED

Then he wrote the word LOVE on a paper

stapled it twenty times

and said

I STAPLE YOU OUT

Editorial Suggestions

Your narrator needs to sound older.

What is he, 8? Could he be more sophisticated?

Does he have attention issues? Do you know who he is?

This book feels a bit adrift. Give us a handle.

We need to walk on that beach.

Does this make sense?

Your time is all over the map.

Is this happening in three weeks? One week?

Do you know where we are?

What is this book really about?

Details drive the action. Don't report on them.

Lead us on. But put a harness on every chapter.

The fishing chapter? They could really

catch a fish. I mean, why not?

The boy's personality needs to be clearer.

He can't be coy.

What is his name again?

We need to fall in love with him.

I'm not sure I even like him.

We need more excitement.

Maybe you could have a stone in every chapter.

Let the stone be the centerpiece. Would that work?

This book will be great.

Dusk

where is the name no one answered to

gone off to live by itself

beneath the pine trees separating houses

without a friend or a bed

without a father to tell it stories

how hard was the path it walked

all those years belonging to none

of our struggles   drifting under

the calendar page elusive as

the river under the floor

when someone said   how have you been

it was strangely that name that tried

to answer

The Mind of Squash

Overnight, & quietly. Beneath the scratchy

leaves we thicken & expand so fast you can't believe.

Sun pours into us but we drink midnight too,

blue locust lullaby feeding our graceful sleep.

When you come back, we are fat. Doubled

in the dark. Faster than you are. Sometimes

we grow together, two of us twining out

from the same stalk, conversational blossoms.

Bring the bucket. Bring the small knife

with the sharp blade. Bring the wind to cool

our wide span of leaves, each one bigger

than a human head, bigger than

dinner plates. Wait till you find the giant prize

we have hidden from you all along—

no muscle-rich upper arm exceeds its size.

But the farmer doesn't like it.

Too big for selling, he says.

Only for zucchini bread.

Never mind. We like it.

We have our own pride.

Necessity Is Only 8 Miles Away

West of Weatherford, Texas,

west of Palo Pinto and Mineral Wells,

west of the red brick highway

and the deserted Baker Hotel

standing watch on its huge emptiness,

is a sign: NECESSITY 8.

It points left.

Left is a small road,

bare branches tangled with snow.

I don't turn.

Something in me swerves, shouts

What is it? What do we need?

but I keep on driving,

past the WATCH FOR ICE bridges,

and the lonely highway patrolmen

with no one to chase,

past Breckenridge to Albany,

small towns fastened like buttons to the plains.

And on, and on, forever, I can see it,

for thousands of miles

we will thread space

with our irregular journeys

stopping now and then

to rest, to wonder

what we always almost find.

Little Blanco River

You're only a foot deep

under green water

your smooth shale skull

is slick & cool

blue dragonfly

skims you like a stone

skipping   skipping

it never goes under

you square-dance with boulders

make a clean swishing sound

centuries of skirts

lifting & falling

in delicate rounds

no one makes a state park out of you

you're not deep enough

little blanco river

don't ever get too big

The Burning House

One night my grandmother and I
left her small apartment stuffed
with folded paper bags
and walked a block to find
the corner blazing

behind the firemen
a knot of huddled neighbors
my grandmother's sheer
speckled dress flaring
so she had to hold it down
with one hand

with the other gripped mine
as the roof
then the second story
then the first story
flames through every window
the tall white house we'd passed
a hundred times on the street where

little happened that was green
or glad

under the city's shadow
the darkness between words
where   the family   what
wind clanking a chain on a fence
till the fireman gave up
and stood beside us on their truck
wiping their faces

we did not know the people
who had lived there
in the last real house
so old it had gas lanterns they said
on the block of gloomy apartments

once there had been houses like that everywhere

there it goes, my grandmother said
as if she had been waiting
for it to go

not even crying

so I stomped my foot

for both of us

Why can't they stop it?

shouting louder till a fireman

turned his sooty gaze

slowly raking the coals

a child who didn't know

how something reaches a point

and passes it

he looked me up and down

then looked away

later there would be nothing

in that spot to say house

no mark of women or cloth or food

no pincushion no hammer

my grandmother still filled

with stories would drop into

a two-year silence

before she died

there were no last words

really

but sometimes far back in her eyes

the flaming layers peeling away

one by one

even the trees of her first small town

curling their leaves

their shade their hopeful rustle

the rest of us standing at a distance

safe

His Life

I don't know what he thinks about.

At night the vault of his face closes up.

He could be underground.

He could be buried treasure.

He could be a donkey trapped in the Bisbee Mine

lowered in so long ago with pulleys and belts, kicking,

till its soft fur faded and eyes went blind.

They made donkeys pull the little carts of ore

from seam to seam.

At night, when the last men stepped

into the creaking lift, the donkeys cried.

Some lived as long as 17 years down there.

The miners still feel bad about it.

They would have hauled them out

to breathe real air in the evenings

but the chute was so deep

and they'd never be able

to force them in again.

Because of Libraries
We Can Say These Things

She is holding the book close to her body,

carrying it home on the cracked sidewalk,

down the tangled hill.

If a dog runs at her again,

she will use the book as a shield.

She looked hard among the long lines

of books to find this one.

When they start talking about money,

when the day contains such long and hot places,

she will go inside.

An orange bed is waiting.

Story without corners.

She will have two families.

They will eat at different hours.

She is carrying a book past the fire station

and the five-and-dime.

What this town has not given her

the book will provide: a sheep,

a wilderness of new solutions.

The book has already lived through its troubles.

The book has a calm cover, a straight spine.

When the step returns to itself

as the best place for sitting

and the old men up and down the street

are latching their clippers,

she will not be alone.

She will have a book to open

and open and open.

Her life starts here.

Cat Plate

That's what we used to do in our house,

says Lydia, when we were mad at our dad—

we served him on the cat plate.

He didn't know, since he never fed the cat.

It made us laugh secretly in the kitchen—

the plate had a crack so maybe

some cat saliva had stuck in there.

It gave us a little buzz.

Once when he was being really mean,

he grabbed what he thought was tuna

in a glass container,

but it was cat food.

Our mother, washing dishes,

froze with her mouth wide open—

I shook my head, finger on my lips.

From the living room he said,

This tuna has taken on a new taste.

No one told him.

We just did our homework silently

at the kitchen table

and grinned when we caught each other's eye.

There were all kinds of ways

we felt better about our lives back then

and sometimes they surprised us.

Famous

The river is famous to the fish.

The loud voice is famous to silence,

which knew it would inherit the earth

before anybody said so.

The cat sleeping on the fence

is famous to the birds

watching him from the birdhouse.

The tear is famous, briefly, to the cheek.

The idea you carry close to your bosom

is famous to your bosom.

The boot is famous to the earth,

more famous than the dress shoe,

which is famous only to floors.

The bent photograph

is famous to the one who carries it

and not at all famous to the one who is pictured.

I want to be famous to shuffling men

who smile while crossing streets,

sticky children in grocery lines,

famous as the one who smiled back.

I want to be famous

in the way a pulley is famous,

or a buttonhole,

not because it did anything spectacular,

but because it never forgot what it could do.

Museum

I was 17, my family had just moved to San Antonio. A local magazine featured an alluring article about a museum called The McNay, an old mansion once the home of an eccentric many-times-married watercolorist named Marian Koogler McNay. She had deeded it to the community to become a museum upon her death. I asked my friend Sally, who drove a cute little convertible, and had moved to Texas a year before we did, if she wanted to go there. Sally said "Sure." She was a good friend that way. We had made up a few words in our own language and could dissolve into laughter just by saying them. Our mothers found us a bit odd. On a sunny Saturday, we drove over to Broadway. Sally asked, "Do you have the address of this place?" "No," I said, "just drive slowly, I'll recognize it, there was a picture in the magazine." I peered in both directions and pointed. "There it is, pull in!" The parking lot under palm trees was nearly empty. We entered, excited. The museum was free. Right away, the spirit of the arched doorways, carved window frames, and elegant artwork overtook us. Sally went left and I went right. A group of people seated in chairs in the lobby stopped talking and stared at us.

"May I help you?" a man said. "No," I said. "We're fine." I didn't like to talk to people in museums. Tours and docents got on my nerves. What if they talked a long time about a painting you weren't interested in? I took a deep breath, moved on to another painting—fireworks over a patio in Mexico, maybe? There weren't very good tags in this museum. In fact, there weren't any. I stood back and gazed. Sally had gone upstairs. The people in the lobby stopped chatting. They seemed nosy, keeping their eyes on me with irritating curiosity. What was their problem? I turned down a hallway. Bougainvillea blooms pressed up right against the windows. Maybe we should have brought a picnic. Where was the Moorish courtyard? I saw some nice sculptures in another room, and a small couch. This would be a good place for reading. Above the couch hung a radiant print by Paul Klee, my favorite artist, blues and pinks merging softly in his own wonderful way. I stepped closer. Suddenly I became aware of a man standing behind me in the doorway. "Where do you think you are?" he asked. I turned sharply. "The McNay Art Museum!" He smiled then, and shook his head. "Sorry to tell you. The McNay is three blocks over, on New Braunfels Street. Take a right when you go out the drive, then another right." "What is this place?" I asked, still confused. He said, "Well, we thought it was our home." My heart jolted. I raced past him to the bottom of the staircase and called out, "Sally! Come down immediately! Urgent!" I remember being tempted to shout something in our private language, but we didn't have a word for this. Sally came to the top of the stairs smiling happily and said, "You HAVE to come up here, there's some really good stuff! And there are old beds too!" "No, Sally, no," I said, as if she were a dog, or a baby. "Come right now. This is an emergency." She stepped elegantly down the stairs in a museum trance, looking puzzled. I just couldn't tell her out loud in front of those people what we had done. I actually pushed her toward the front door, waving my hand at the family in the chairs, saying, "Sorry, ohmygod, please forgive us, you have a really nice place." Sally stared at me outside. When I told her, she covered her mouth and doubled over with laughter, shaking. We were still in their yard. I imagined them inside looking out the windows at us. She couldn't believe how long they let us look around without saying anything, either. "That was really friendly of them!" "Get in the car," I said sternly. "This is mortifying."

The real McNay was splendid, but we felt a little nervous the whole time we were there. Van Gogh, Picasso, Gauguin, Tamayo. This time, there were tags. This time we stayed together, in case anything else weird happened.

We never told anyone.

Thirty years later, a nice-looking woman approached me in a public place. "Excuse me," she said. "I need to ask a strange question. Did you ever, by any chance, enter a residence, long ago, thinking it was the McNay Museum?"
Thirty years later, my cheeks still burned. "Yes. But how do you know? I never told anyone."
"That was my home. I was a teenager sitting with my family talking in the living room. Before you came over, I never realized what a beautiful place I lived in. I never felt lucky before. You thought it was a museum. My feelings changed about my parents after that. They had good taste! I have always wanted to thank you."

Little Boys Running on the Dock

Seagulls startle, soar,

a massive flapping,

and the boys call out,

Sorry, pigeons!

One Boy Told Me

Music lives inside my legs.
It's coming out when I talk.

I'm going to send my valentines
to people you don't even know.

Oatmeal cookies make my throat gallop.

Grown-ups keep their feet on the ground
when they swing. I hate that.

Look at those 2 O's with a smash in the middle—
that spells good-bye.

Don't ever say "purpose" again,
let's throw the word out.

Don't talk big to me.
I'm carrying my box of faces.
If I want to change faces, I will.

Yesterday faded

but tomorrow's in **BOLDFACE**.

When I grow up my old names

will live in the house

where we live now.

I'll come and visit them.

Only one of my eyes is tired.

The other eye and my body aren't.

Is it true all metal was liquid first?

Does that mean if we bought our car earlier

they could have served it

in a cup?

There's a stopper in my arm

that's not going to let me grow any bigger.

I'll be like this always, small.

And I will be deep water too.

Wait. Just wait. How deep is the river?

Would it cover the tallest man with his hands in the air?

Your head is a souvenir.

When you were in New York I could see you
in real life walking in my mind.

I'll invite a bee to live in your shoe.
What if you found your shoe
full of honey?

What if the clock said 6:92
instead of 6:30? Would you be scared?

My tongue is the car wash
for the spoon.

Can noodles swim?

My toes are dictionaries.
Do you need any words?

From now on I'll only drink white milk
on January 26.

What does minus mean?

I never want to minus you.

Just think – no one has ever seen

inside this peanut before!

It is hard being a person.

I do and don't love you—

isn't that happiness?

(Exact recorded quotes from Madison Cloudfeather Nye, Ages 2 and 3)

How Far Is It to the Land We Left?

On the first day of his life

the baby opens his eyes

and gets tired doing even that.

He cries when they place a cap on his head.

Too much, too much!

Later the whole world will touch him

and he won't even flinch.

Something Forgotten

This morning an Amish farmer awakens with furrowed fields

   spread ready before him   his wife stirring molasses

     two young sons   giggling in a bedroom as they tie on
their boots

          what the world looks like to them

  Do they feel planted at the center of a thought or somewhere
out on a rim?

I'm thinking of the server who said every morning   *I am not
really a waitress*

     I am a photographer   *just doing this to help out a
friend*

  And the 5th grade girl in a tiny town   Eastern Shore
Maryland

   who read a poem so perfectly in Spanish   twice   to her

rapt classmates

each syllable rippled

when she said she plans to be a translator   everyone
clapped

In another school   rainbowed mural in hall
WE ARE ALL WONDERS

such simple words   I could have stood there weeping

invisible among kids   till the whole place emptied

These days there are men and women   who seem to have
forgotten
humility

For the rest of us to feel lost   is not the worst thing

The Traveling Onion

It is believed that the onion originally came from India. In Egypt it was an object of worship ... From Egypt the onion entered Greece and on to Italy, thence into all of Europe.

—Better Living Cookbook

When I think how far the onion has traveled

just to enter my stew today, I could kneel and praise

all small forgotten miracles,

crackly paper peeling on the drainboard,

pearly layers in smooth agreement,

the way knife enters onion

and onion falls apart on the chopping block,

a history revealed.

And I would never scold the onion

for causing tears.

It is right that tears fall

for something small and forgotten.

How at meal, we sit to eat,

commenting on herbal aroma,

but never on the translucence of onion,

now limp, now divided,

or its traditionally honorable career:

For the sake of others,

disappear.

The Lost Parrot

Carlos bites the end of his pencil

He's trying to write a dream-poem

But waves at me, frowning

I had a parrot

He talks slowly, his voice

travels far to get out of his body

A dream-parrot?

No, a real parrot!

Write about it

He squirms, looks nervous

everyone else is almost finished

and he hasn't started

It left

What left?

The parrot

He hunches over the table

pencil gripped in fist

shaping the heavy letters

Days later we will write

story-poems, sound-poems

but always the same subject for Carlos

It left

He will insist on reading it

and the class will look puzzled

The class is tired of this parrot

> *Write more, Carlos*
>
> *I can't*
>
> *Why not?*
>
> *I don't know   where   it went*

Each day when I leave

he stares at the ceiling

Maybe he is planning an expedition

into the back streets of San Antonio

armed with nets and ripe mangoes

He will find the parrot nesting

in a rain gutter

This time he will guard it carefully

make sure it stays

Before winter comes

and his paper goes white

in all directions

Before anything else he loves

gets away

THE HOLY LAND
THAT ISN'T

Before You Can

My Jewish friends are kind and gentle.
Not one of them would harm another person
even if they didn't know that person.

My Arab friends are kind and gentle.
Not one of them would harm another person
even if they didn't know that person.
They might press you to drink 45 small cups
of coffee or tea, but that would be all.

My Jewish friends have never taken my house,
my land, herded me into a cell, tortured me,
cut down my tree, never once.
My Arab friends have never built a bomb.

We respect each other as equals.

We look somewhat alike.

We laugh similarly.

We have never said the other should not exist.

So where is the problem exactly?
Let's be specific. Who and where and what
is the problem exactly? You have to know
before you can fix it.

Blood

"A true Arab knows how to catch
a fly in his hands,"
my father would say. And he'd prove it,
cupping the buzzer instantly
while the host with the swatter stared.

In the spring our palms peeled.
True Arabs believed watermelon
could heal fifty ways.
I changed these to fit the occasion.

Years before, a girl knocked,
wanted to see the Arab.
I said we didn't have one.
After that, my father told more stories,
"Shihab"—"shooting star"—
a good name, borrowed from the sky.
Once I said, "When we die, we give it back?"
He said that's what a true Arab would say.

Today the headlines clot in my blood.
A Palestinian boy dangles a toy truck
on the front page.
Homeless fig, this tragedy with a terrible root
is too big for us. What flag can we wave?
I wave the flag of stone and seed,
table mat stitched in blue.

I call my father, we talk around the news.
It is too much for him,
neither of his two languages can reach it.
I drive into the country to find sheep, cows,
to plead with the air:
who calls anyone *civilized?*
Where can the crying heart graze?
What does a true Arab do now?

My Father and the Figtree

For other fruits my father was indifferent.

He'd point at the cherry trees and say,

"See those? I wish they were figs."

In the evenings he sat by our beds

weaving folktales like vivid little scarves.

They always involved a figtree.

Even when it didn't fit, he'd stick it in.

Once Joha was walking down the road

and he saw a figtree.

Or, he tied his donkey to a figtree

and went to sleep.

Or, later when they caught and arrested him,

his pockets were full of figs.

At age six, I ate a dried fig and shrugged.

"That's not what I'm talking about!" he said.

"I'm talking about a fig straight from the earth—

gift of Allah!—on a branch so heavy it touches the ground.

I'm talking about picking the largest fattest sweetest fig

in the world and putting it in my mouth."

(Here he'd stop and close his eyes.)

Years passed, we lived in many houses, none had figtrees.

We had lima beans, zucchini, parsley, beets.

"Plant one!" my mother said, but my father never did.

He tended garden half-heartedly, forgot to water,

let the okra get too big.

"What a dreamer he is. Look how many things he starts

and doesn't finish."

The last time he moved, I got a phone call.

My father, in Arabic, chanting a song I'd never heard.

"What's that?"

"Wait till you see!"

He took me out to the new yard.

There, in the middle of Dallas, Texas,

a tree with the largest, fattest, sweetest figs in the world.

"It's a figtree song!" he said,

plucking his fruits like ripe tokens,

emblems, assurance

of a world that was always his own.

Arabic Coffee

It was never too strong for us,

make it blacker, Papa,

thick in the bottom,

tell again how years will gather

in small white cups,

how luck lives in a spot of grounds.

Leaning over the stove, he let it

boil to the top and down again.

Two times. No sugar in his pot.

And the place where men and women

break off from one another

was not present in that room.

The hundred disappointments,

fire swallowing olive-wood beads

at the warehouse, and the dreams

tucked like pocket handkerchiefs

into each day, took their places

on the table, near the half-empty

dish of corn. And none were
more important than the others,
and all were guests. When
he carried the tray into the room,
high and balanced in his hands,
it was an offering to all of them,
stay, be seated, follow the talk
wherever it goes. The coffee was
the center of the flower.
Like clothes on a line saying
You will live long enough to wear me,
a motion of faith. There is this,
and there is more.

Red Brocade

The Arabs used to say

When a stranger appears at your door,

feed him for three days

before asking who he is,

where he's come from,

where he's headed.

That way, he'll have strength

enough to answer.

Or, by then you'll be

such good friends

you don't care.

Let's go back to that.

Rice? Pine nuts?

Here, take the red brocade pillow.

My child will serve water

to your horse.

No, I was not busy when you came!
I was not preparing to be busy.
That's the armor everyone put on
to pretend they had a purpose
in the world.

I refuse to be claimed.
Your plate is waiting.
We will snip fresh mint
into your tea.

During a War

Best wishes to you & yours,
he closes the letter.
For a moment I can't
fold it up again—
where does "yours" end?
Dark eyes pleading
what could we have done
differently?
Your family,
your community,

circle of earth, we did not want,

we tried to stop,

we were not heard

by dark eyes who are dying

now. How easily they

would have welcomed us in

for coffee, serving it

in a simple room

with a radiant rug.

Your friends & mine.

For Mohammed Zeid of Gaza, Age 15

There is no *stray* bullet, sirs.

no bullet like a worried cat

crouching under a bush,

no half-hairless puppy bullet

dodging midnight streets.

The bullet could not be a pecan

plunking the tin roof,

not hardly, no fluff of pollen

on October's breath,

no humble pebble at our feet.

So don't gentle it, please.

We live among stray thoughts,

tasks abandoned midstream.

Our fickle hearts are fat

with stray devotions,

we feel at home

among bits and pieces,

the wandering ways of words.

But this bullet had no innocence, did not

wish anyone well, you can't tell us otherwise

by naming it mildly, this bullet was never the friend

of life, should not be granted immunity

by soft saying—*friendly fire, straying death-eye,*

why have we given the wrong weight to what we do?

Mohammed, Mohammed, deserves the truth.

This bullet had no secret happy hopes,

it was not singing to itself with eyes closed

under the bridge.

The Day

I missed the day

on which it was said

others should not have

certain weapons, but we could.

Not only could, but should,

and do.

I missed that day.

Was I sleeping?

I might have been digging

in the yard,

doing something small and slow

as usual.

Or maybe I wasn't born yet.

What about all the other people

who aren't born?

Who will tell them?

Everything in Our World
Did Not Seem to Fit

Once they started invading us, taking our houses

and trees, drawing lines, pushing us into tiny places.

It wasn't a bargain or deal or even a real war.

To this day they pretend it was.

But it was something else.

We were sorry what happened to them but

we had nothing to do with it.

You don't think what a little plot of land means

till someone takes it and you can't go back.

Your feet still want to walk there.

Now you are drifting worse

than homeless dust, very lost feeling.

I cried even to think of our hallway,

cool stone passage inside the door.

Nothing would fit for years.

They came with guns, uniforms, declarations.

Life magazine said,

"It was surprising to find some Arabs still in their houses."

Surprising? Where else would we be?

Up on the hillsides?

Conversing with mint and sheep, digging in dirt?

Why was someone else's need for a home

greater than our own need for our own homes

we were already living in? No one has ever been able

to explain this sufficiently. But they find

a lot of other things to talk about.

Pictures from the Occupied Territories

Faces under occupation

carry a different light

than ones used to being

welcomed. Quiet shine,

the undersides of leaves.

Intricate traceries

of work done in secret.

Consider the steady gaze

of constellations

forming complete images,

radiating in place,

whether or not

we give them names.

My Grandmother in the Stars

It is possible we will not meet again
on earth. To think this fills my throat
with dust. Then there is only the sky
tying the universe together.

Just now the neighbor's horse must be standing
patiently, hoof on stone, waiting for his day
to open. What you think of him,
and the village's one heroic cow,
is the knowledge I wish to gather.
I bow to your rugged feet,
the moth-eaten scarves that knot your hair.

Where we live in the world

is never one place. Our hearts,

those dogged mirrors, keep flashing us

moons before we are ready for them.

You and I on a roof at sunset,

our two languages adrift,

heart saying, Take this home with you,

never again,

and only memory making us rich.

It is not a game, it was never a game

It was a girl's arm, the right one

that held a pencil.

She liked her arm.

It was a small stone house

with an iron terrace,

flower pot beside the door.

People passing,

loaves of bread,

little plans

the size of a thought,

dropping off something

you borrowed,

buying a small sack of *zaater*,

it was a hand with fingers

dipping the scoop into the barrel.

I will not live this way,

said a woman with a baby on her hip,

but she was where she was.

These men do not represent me,

said the teacher with her students

in pressed blue smocks.

They had sharpened their pencils.

Desks lined in a simple room.

It was school,

numbers on a page,

a radiant sky with clouds.

In the old days you felt happy to see it.

No one wanted anything

to drop out of it

except rain. Where was rain?

It was not a game, it was

unbelievable sorrow

and fear.

A hand that a mother held.

A pocket. A glass.

It was not war.

It was people.

We had gone nowhere

in a million years.

What Kind of Fool Am I?

He sang with abandon,

combing his black, black hair.

Each morning in the shower,

first in Arabic, rivery ripples

of song carrying him back

to his first beloved land,

then in English, where his repertoire

was short. *No kind at all!* we'd shout,

throwing ourselves into the brisk arc

of his cologne for a morning kiss.

But he gave us freedom to be fools

if we needed to, which we certainly

would later, which we all do now and then,

perhaps a father's greatest gift—

that blessing.

Every day was your birthday

If light fell gently onto the windowsill

If no one you knew was teargassed

If the children came home from school
swinging their bookbags

and sat laughing
books in laps
to do the work
you had never learned
how to do

that was a good day

Sitti placed a cut onion to her face
to temper the fumes
whispering

Tell this to the soldiers

I was born in the sliver of time

the smallest eye of the apricot

the ripple of days one to another

cast upon wind in a far place

Don't know its name

Maybe 5 kilometers from here

There was a well my mother drank from

on the night I was born

I think there were horses

If you want to celebrate me

Start everywhere

Before I Was a Gazan

I was a boy

and my homework was missing,

paper with numbers on it,

stacked and lined,

I was looking for my piece of paper,

proud of this plus that, then multiplied,

not remembering if I had left it

on the table after showing to my uncle

or the shelf after combing my hair

but it was still somewhere

and I was going to find it and turn it in,

make my teacher happy,

make her say my name to the whole class,

before everything got subtracted

in a minute

even my uncle

even my teacher

even the best math student and his baby sister

who couldn't talk yet.

And now I would do anything

for a problem I could solve.

Double Peace

For Yehuda Amichai

Not for him and his people alone

    But for all who loved that rocky land

Everybody   everybody   Sing it!

No chosen and unchosen but everybody chosen

      Sing it!

All families living under tiled rooftops

Or flat roofs with strung clotheslines

    T-shirts   bedsheets   flags of surrender

I show you my cloth   I live the way you live

All the cousins   second cousins

    extra cousins   unknown cousins

No choice   everyone a cousin

  peace better than hurtful moves

    better better sing it!

Not rain that fell on a few houses only

    Not sun that shone on a few favored yards

Not air in small containers only for some lungs

    Double peace multiplied

Outside   inside   every ancient space

  every sleek new room with tall windows

Peace for sheep and goats grazing in meadows

  (They already have it)

  Peace for buckets waiting on doorsteps

Peace for brown eggs lined on counters waiting to be

    cracked

   Peace in skillets and spatulas

We met at the corner   went to his home for breakfast

stared out the window together   the shining city

   the sorrowing city

He said, I would never have taken your father's home!

I could never have lived in a stolen Arab home!

The great voice of the Jewish people said this to my face

  our conversation

   where streets converged

Amir & Anna

"It's unbelievable, this cycle of violence, and how neither party realizes they're both losing."

—Dr. Cairo Arafat, West Bank

Amir can't sleep.

He dives under his bed.

Anna is afraid of everything.

Parked cars, moving buses.

Anna is afraid of toast.

Their names begin with "A,"

contain the same number of letters.

They live one mile apart.

No one has given them

what they deserve.

Around both their houses,

all the Arab and Jewish houses,

red poppies sleep beneath

dirt and stones.

What do they know?

In March green spokes

with fluttering heads

rise and rise on every side.

Jerusalem

"Let's be the same wound if we must bleed.
Let's fight side by side, even if the enemy
Is ourselves. I am yours, you are mine."

—*Tommy Olofsson*

I'm not interested in

who suffered the most.

I'm interested in

people getting over it.

Once when my father was a boy

a stone hit him on the head.

Hair would never grow there.

Our fingers found the tender spot

and its riddle: the boy who has fallen

stands up. A bucket of pears

in his mother's doorway welcomes him home.

The pears are not crying.

Later his friend who threw the stone

says he was aiming at a bird.

And my father starts growing wings.

Each carries a tender spot:

something our lives forgot to give us.

A man builds a house and says,

"I am native now."

A woman speaks to a tree

in place of her son.

And olives come.

A child's poem says,

"I don't like wars,

they end up with monuments."

He's painting a bird with wings

wide enough to cover two roofs at once.

Why are we so monumentally slow?

Soldiers stalk a pharmacy:

big guns, little pills.

If you tilt your head just slightly,

it's ridiculous.

There's a place in this brain

where hate won't grow.

I touch its riddle: wind, and seeds.

Something pokes us as we sleep.

It's late but everything comes next.

PEOPLE ARE THE
ONLY HOLY LAND

Two Countries

Skin remembers how long the years grow

when skin is not touched, gray tunnel

of singleness, feather lost from the tail

of a bird, swirling onto a step,

swept away by someone who never saw

it was a feather. Skin ate, walked,

slept by itself, knew how to raise

a see-you-later hand. But skin felt

it was never seen, never known as

a land on the map, nose like a city,

hip like a city, gleaming dome of the mosque

and the hundred corridors of cinnamon and rope.

Skin had hope, that's what skin does.

Heals over the scarred place, makes a road.

Love means you breathe in two countries.

And skin remembers, silk, spiny grass,

deep in the pocket that is skin's secret own.

Even now, when skin is not alone,

it remembers being alone

and thanks something larger

that there are travelers,

that people go places

bigger than themselves.

Wedding Cake

Once on a plane
a woman asked me to hold her baby
and disappeared.
I figured it was safe,
our being on a plane and all.
How far could she go?

She returned one hour later,
having changed her clothes
and washed her hair.
I didn't recognize her.

By this time the baby
and I had examined
each other's necks.
We had cried a little.
I had a silver bracelet
and a watch.
Gold studs glittered
in the baby's ears.

She wore a tiny white dress
leafed with layers
like a wedding cake.

I did not want
to give her back.

The baby's curls coiled tightly
against her scalp,
another alphabet.
I read *new new new.*
My mother gets tired.
I'll chew your hand.

The baby left my skirt crumpled,
my lap aching.
Now I'm her secret guardian,
the little nub of dream
that rises slightly
but won't come clear.

As she grows,

as she feels ill at ease,

I'll bob my knee.

What will she forget?

Whom will she marry?

He'd better check with me.

I'll say once she flew

dressed like a cake

between two doilies of cloud.

She could slip the card into a pocket,

pull it out.

Already she knew the small finger

was funnier than the whole arm.

So Much Happiness

For Michael

It is difficult to know what to do with so much happiness.

With sadness there is something to rub against,

a wound to tend with lotion and cloth.

When the world falls in around you, you have pieces to pick up,

something to hold in your hands, like ticket stubs, or change.

But happiness floats.

It doesn't need you to hold it down.

It doesn't need anything.

Happiness lands on the roof of the next house, singing,

and disappears when it wants to.

You are happy either way.

Even the fact that you once lived in a peaceful tree house

and now live over a quarry of noise and dust

cannot make you unhappy.

Everything has a life of its own,

it too could wake up filled with possibilities

of coffee cake and ripe peaches,

and love even the floor which needs to be swept,

the soiled linens and scratched records . . .

Since there is no place large enough

to contain so much happiness,

you shrug, you raise your hands, and it flows out of you

into everything you touch. You are not responsible.

You take no credit, as the night sky takes no credit

for the moon, but continues to hold it, and share it,

and in that way, be known.

San Antonio

Tonight I lingered over your name,

the delicate assembly of vowels

a voice inside my head.

You were sleeping when I arrived.

I stood by your bed

and watched the sheets rise gently.

I knew how you would moan,

what slant of light

might make you turn over.

It was then I felt

the highways slide out of my hands.

I remembered the old men

in the west side café

dealing dominoes like magical charms.

It was then I knew,

like a woman looking backwards,

I could not leave you

or find anyone I loved more.

United

When sleepless, it's helpful to meditate

on mottoes of the states.

South Carolina, "While I breathe I hope."

Perhaps this could be

the new flag on the empty flagpole.

Or "I direct" from Maine—

Why, because Maine gets the first sunrise?

How bossy, Maine!

In Arkansas, "The People Rule." Lucky you!

Kansas, "To the Stars Through Difficulties"—

clackety wagon wheels, long land,

and the droning press of heat—cool stars, relief.

Idaho, "Let it be perpetual"—now this is strange.

Idaho, what is your "it"?

Who chose these lines?

How many contenders?

What would my motto be tonight, in tangled sheets?

Texas, "Friendship," now boasts

    the Open Carry Law.

Wisconsin, where my mother's parents are buried,
chose "Forward."
Washington, wisest, "By and By."
New Mexico, "It grows as it goes"—
now this is scary. Two dangling *its*.
This does not represent that glorious place.
West Virginia, "Mountaineers are always free"—
really?
Oklahoma must be tired, "Labor conquers all things."
Oklahoma, get together with Nevada, who chose
only "Industry" as motto.
I think of Nevada as a playground,
or mostly empty. How wrong we are
about one another.
For Alaska to pick "North to the Future"
seems odd. Where else are they going?

Pause

The boy needed
to stop by the road.
What pleasure to let
the engine quit droning
inside the long heat,
to feel where they were.
Sometimes
she was struck by this
as if a plank had slapped
the back of her head.

They were thirsty
as grasses
leaning sideways
in the ditch,
Big Bluestem
and Little Barley,
Texas Cupgrass,
Hairy Crabgrass,

Green Sprangletop.
She could stop at a store
selling only grass names
and be happy.

They would pause
and the pause
seep into them,
fence post,
twisted wire,
brick chimney
without its house,
pollen taking flight
toward the cities.

Something would gather
back into place.
Take the word "home"
for example,
often considered
to have an address.
How it could sweep across you,

miles beyond the last

neat packages of ice,

and nothing be wider

than its pulse.

Out here,

everywhere,

the boy looking away from her

across the fields.

Bill's Beans

For William Stafford

Under the leaves, they're long and curling.

I pull a perfect question mark and two lean twins,

feeling the magnetic snap of stem, the ripened weight.

At the end of a day, the earth smells thirsty.

He left his brown hat, his shovel and his pen.

I don't know how deep bean roots go.

We could experiment.

He left the sky over Oregon, the fluent trees.

He gave us our lives that were hiding under our feet

saying, You know what to do.

So we'll take these beans

back into the house and steam them.

We'll eat them one by one with our fingers,

the clean click and freshness.

We'll thank him forever for our breath,

and the brevity of bean.

Alphabet

One by one
the old people
of our neighborhood
are going up
into the air

Their yards still wear
small white narcissus
sweetening winter

their stones
glisten
under the sun
but one by one
we are losing
their housecoats
their formal phrasings
their cupcakes

When I string their names

on the long cord

when I think how

there is almost no one left

who remembers

what stood in that

brushy spot

ninety years ago

when I pass their yards

and the bare peach tree

bends a little

when I see their rusted chairs

sitting in the same spots

what will be forgotten

falls over me

like the sky

over our whole neighborhood

or the time my plane

circled high above our street

the roof of our house

dotting the tiniest

"i"

Lying While Birding

Yes   Yes

    I see it

so they won't keep telling you

    where it is

At Portales, New Mexico

They spoke of tumbleweeds
coming to their doors in the night,
whole herds of them scooting across the desert,
arriving at any place there was a wall,
and staying.
In the morning they would rise
to find them stacked,
grazing on air.

Their neighbor tried fire
but his living room went up in flames.
You couldn't fit a tumbleweed in a garbage sack
unless it was a baby one.
If you swept them across the street,
they would return to you, loyal,
on the next powerful gust.

What did people do to protect their homes
in New Mexico?
At night they dreamed eastern hedges
guarded their beds,
steady lamplight palming each roof.
They never knew they would be planted
on this thin blue line,
nothing between themselves and the next town
but a sign for Indian Gifts.

Where they grew up a root meant something.
Trees lived a hundred years
and bulbs slept secure in the ground.
But here in the west,
the days were flat tables spread with wind,
you never knew who was coming,
how many places to set for dinner,
they had imagined a knock
and opened the door for four big ones,
rolling, right up to the chairs.

You never knew how far your voice would travel

once you let a word out,

felt that curled stem shrinking in your throat

and the thousand directions it could

or could not go.

Nez Perce

Their silence

is larger

than our silence.

I Still Have Everything You Gave Me

It is dusty on the edges.

Slightly rotten.

I guard it without thinking.

Focus on it once a year
when I shake it out in the wind.

I do not ache.

I would not trade.

If the Shoe Doesn't Fit

you take it off

of course you take it off

it doesn't worry you

it isn't your shoe

Tassajara

The beauty of yes

the beauty of no

shining moments

wearing different clothes

Valentine for Ernest Mann

You can't order a poem like you order a taco.
Walk up to the counter, say, "I'll take two,"
and expect it to be handed back to you
on a shiny plate.

Still, I like your spirit.
Anyone who says, "Here's my address,
write me a poem," deserves something in reply.
So I'll tell a secret instead:
poems hide. In the bottoms of our shoes,
they are sleeping. They are the shadows
drifting across our ceilings the moment
before we wake up. What we have to do
is live in a way that lets us find them.

Once I knew a man who gave his wife
two skunks for a valentine.
He couldn't understand why she was crying.
"I thought they had such beautiful eyes."

And he was serious. He was a serious man
who lived in a serious way. Nothing was ugly
just because the world said so. He really
liked those skunks. So, he re-invented them
as valentines and they became beautiful.
At least, to him. And the poems that had been hiding
in the eyes of skunks for centuries
crawled out and curled up at his feet.

Maybe if we re-invent whatever our lives give us
we find poems. Check your garage, the odd sock
in your drawer, the person you almost like, but not quite.
And let me know.

The Young Poets of Winnipeg

scurried around a classroom papered with poems.

Even the ceiling, pink and orange quilts of phrase . . .

they introduced one another, perched on a tiny stage

to read their work, blessed their teacher who

encouraged them to stretch, wouldn't let their parents

attend the reading because parents might criticize,

believed in the third and fourth eyes, the eyes in

the undersides of leaves, the polar bears

a thousand miles north,

and sprouts of grass under the snow. They knew their poems

were glorious, that second-graders could write better

than third or fourth, because of what happened

on down the road, the measuring sticks

that came out of nowhere, poking and channeling

the view, the way fences broke up winter,

or driveways separated the smooth white sheets

birds wrote on with their feet.

The Shopper

I visit the grocery store

like the Indian woman in Peru

attends the cathedral.

Saying a few words over and over;

butter, bread, apples, butter   bread   apples.

I nod to the grandmothers muttering among roots.

Their carts tell stories: they eat little, they live alone.

Last week two women compared their cancers

matter-of-factly as I compare soups.

How do you reach that point of acceptance?

Life and death shoved in the same basket

and you with a calm face waiting at the checkout stand.

We must bless ourselves with peaches.

Pray to the eggplant, silent among her sisters,

that the seeds will not be bitter on the tongue.

Confess our fears to the flesh of tomato:

we too go forward only halfway ripened

dreaming of the deeper red.

The Art of Disappearing

When they say, Don't I know you?
say no.

When they invite you to the party,
remember what parties are like
before answering.
Someone telling you in a loud voice
they once wrote a poem.
Greasy sausage balls on a paper plate.
Then reply.

If they say We should get together
say why?

It's not that you don't love them anymore.
You're trying to remember something
too important to forget.
Trees. The monastery bell at twilight.
Tell them you have a new project.
It will never be finished.

When someone recognizes you in a grocery store

nod briefly and become a cabbage.

When someone you haven't seen in ten years

appears at the door,

don't start singing him all your new songs.

You will never catch up.

Walk around feeling like a leaf.

Know you could tumble any second.

Then decide what to do with your time.

Missing the Boat

It is not so much that the boat passed
and you failed to notice it.
It is more like the boat stopping
directly outside your bedroom window,
the captain blowing the signal-horn,
band playing a rousing march.
The boat shouted, waving bright flags,
its silver hull blinding in the sunlight.

But you had this idea
you were going by train.
You kept checking the timetable,
digging for tracks.

And the boat got tired of you,

so tired it pulled up its anchor

and raised the ramp.

The boat bobbed into the distance,

shrinking like a toy—

at which point you probably realized

you had always loved the sea.

Feeling Wise

A lady was quoted in the newspaper.

"It is not so hard to feel wise.

Just think of something dumb you could say,

Then don't say it."

I like her.

I would take her gingerbread

if I knew where her house was.

Julia Child the famous chef said,

"I never feel lonely in the kitchen.

Food is very friendly.

Just looking at a potato, I like

to pat it."

Staring down,

you feel tall.

Staring into someone else's eyes,

you're not alone.

Staring out the window during school,

you become the future,

smooth and large.

Mysterious World

My grandparents sold
their old gray house in Illinois
with everything in it.

Sewing machines, piano, rocking chair.
Till now, the attic packed with their receipts.

My father died with his head
full of stories, hopes, a perfect command
of two languages.

I'm standing by a creek that sends
everything it knows downstream.

Three Hundred Goats

In icy fields.

Is water flowing in the tank?

(Is it the year of the sheep or the goat?

   Chinese zodiac inconclusive . . .)

Will they huddle together, warm bodies pressing?

O lead them to a secluded corner,

little ones toward bulkier mothers.

Lead them to the brush, which cuts the wind.

Another frigid night swooping down—

Aren't you worried about them? I ask my friend

who lives by herself on the ranch of goats,

far from here near the town of Ozona.

She shrugs, "Not really,

They know what to do. They're *goats*."

Storyteller

Where is the door to the story?
Is the door left open?

When he sat by our beds,
the day rushed past like water.

Driftwood, bricks,
heavy cargoes disappearing downstream,

no matter, no matter,
even the trees outside our screens

tipped their cooling leaves to listen.
We swam so easily

to the stone village,
women in thick dresses,

men with smoky breath,

sat around the fire pitching in

our own twigs,

the world curled around us,

sizzled and popped.

We dropped our troubles

into the lap of the storyteller

and they turned into someone else's.

Burlington, Vermont

In the lovely free public library

only library I ever met

that loans out garden tools

as well as books

rakes & long-handled clippers

from large buckets by the counter

I sat in a peaceful room

with people I will never know

reading about far-away war

war I am paying for

war I don't want & never wanted

& put my head down

on the smooth wooden table

wishing to weep loudly or quietly

it did not matter

in the purifying presence

of women & men

shovels & hoes

devoted to growing

I Don't Know

If my father can hear me. But it is important to pretend he can.

My sanity rests in that. The man he was can hear the girl I am.

Mom Gives Away Your Ties

Just last week, nearly three years since you flew

from your miserable precious body,

I buried my face in your ties.

The dark blue Peruvian

with the little white llama.

They seemed comfortable together,

still hanging on the inside of your closet door,

mark of a man, family of shiny colors and stripes,

journalist, diplomat ties,

ties that said, *We will be hopeful*

in the workplace even when we hate what we

are doing, or *Cologne helps a man*

survive, fragrant still as your cheek

every morning of my own young world.

I thought of taking some but liked them there

in place, where you left them,

so today when I heard they'd been given

to a raggedy swap shop near a lake,

I had to stand outside a long time

in the huge air, your one real home

for all the days you walked among us.

A Few Questions for Bashar Assad

We're curious about your shoes, whether they retain laces

of a traditional kind or you now prefer slip-ons. Do they sit,

buffed leather, beside your wardrobe at night?

Did you glance out the window today or place a hand

on the head of your child within the last 24 hours?

Can you recall exactly what that child said to you or asked?

If you made any kind of promise?

Was it less a conversation than a comfort,

something a parent mumbles

as the family circles and dines, tucks in and abides?

Was today's breakfast predetermined, a usual menu, or food

you requested on the spot? Do you love labneh?

Anything in that meal to be peeled, perhaps?

And who peeled it?

Are there any burned-out bulbs in your beautiful lamps?

Once in Homs, some of us purchased pistachios,

weighed in an old balance-scale, coned into brown paper bag

with the top folded over. The grinning vendor

poured in extra, touched his forehead.

Those nuts tasted smoky for two hundred miles.

Did you ever purchase anything in Homs

and like the person who sold it to you?

What about Aleppo? Did you love Aleppo?

Are you sleeping enough, can you remember

the time before you were bigger than a man,

have those days dissolved,

did you ever taste the water at Ma'alula from the miracle spring

in a cave, the water said to bring faithful people

whatever they wish for, is it still flowing, do you know?

Rain

A teacher asked Paul
what he would remember
from third grade, and he sat
a long time before writing
"this year sumbody tutched me
on the shoulder"
and turned his paper in.
Later she showed it to me,
gloomily.
The words he wrote were large
as houses in a landscape.
He wanted to go inside them
and live, he could fill in
the windows of "o" and "d"
and be safe while outside
birds building nests in drainpipes
knew nothing of the coming rain.

Shoulders

A man crosses the street in rain,

stepping gently, looking two times north and south,

because his son is asleep on his shoulder.

No car must splash him.

No car drive too near to his shadow.

This man carries the world's most sensitive cargo

but he's not marked.

Nowhere does his jacket say FRAGILE,

HANDLE WITH CARE.

His ear fills up with breathing.

He hears the hum of a boy's dream

deep inside him.

We're not going to be able

to live in this world

if we're not willing to do what he's doing

with one another.

The road will only be wide.
The rain will never stop falling.

Hummingbird

"The world is big and I want to have a good look at it before it gets dark."
—*John Muir*

Lyda Rose asked, "Are you a grown-up?"

The most flattering question of my adult life.

She darted around me like a hummingbird,

knotted in gauzy pink scarves,

braiding thyme into my hair.

There, on the brink of summer,

all summers blurred.

"No," I said.

"I don't think so.

I don't want to be."

"What are you then?"

Her dog snored by the couch,

little sister dozed on a pillow.

When her mom came home, we'd drink hot tea,

talk about our dead fathers, and cry.

"I think I'm a turtle," I said. "Hibernating.

And a mouse in the moss.

And sometimes a hummingbird like you."

She jumped on my stomach then.

Asked if I'd ever worn a tutu

like the frayed pink one

she favored the whole spring.

No, not that.

"I have a shovel, though," I said.

"For digging in the garden every night

before dark. And a small piano like yours

that pretends to be a harpsichord.

And I really love my broom."

What Is Supposed to Happen

When you were small,

we watched you sleeping,

waves of breath

filling your chest.

Sometimes we hid behind

the wall of baby, soft cradle

of baby needs.

I loved carrying you between

my own body and the world.

Now you are sharpening pencils,

entering the forest of

lunch boxes, little desks.

People I never saw before

call out your name

and you wave.

This loss I feel,

this shrinking,

as your field of roses

grows and grows . . .

Now I understand history.

Now I understand my mother's

ancient eyes.

Alive

Dear Abby, said someone from Oregon,

I am having trouble with my boyfriend's attachment

to an ancient gallon of milk still full

in his refrigerator. I told him it's me or the milk,

is this unreasonable? Dear Carolyn,

my brother won't speak to me

because fifty years ago I whispered

a monkey would kidnap him in the night

to take him back to his true family,

but he should have known it was a joke

when it didn't happen, don't you think?

Dear Board of Education, no one will ever

remember a test. Repeat. Stories,

poems, projects, experiments,

mischief, yes, but never a test.

Dear Dog Behind the Fence, you really need

to calm down now. You have been barking

every time I walk to the compost for two years

and I have not robbed your house. Relax.

When I asked the man on the other side

if you bother him too, he smiled and said no,

he makes me feel less alone. Should I be more

worried about the dog or the man?

You Are Your Own State Department

Each day I miss Japanese precision. Trying to arrange things

the way they would. And I miss the call to prayer

at Sharjah, the large collective pause.   Or

the shy strawberry vendor with rickety wooden cart,

single small lightbulb pointed at a mound of berries.

In one of China's great cities, before dawn.

Forever I miss my Arab father's way with mint leaves

floating in a cup of sugared tea—his delicate hands

arranging rinsed figs on a plate. What have we here?

said the wolf in the children's story

stumbling upon people doing kind, small things.

Is this small monster one of us?

When your country does not feel cozy, what do you do?

Teresa walks more now, to feel closer to her

ground. If destination within two miles, she must

hike or take the bus. Carries apples,

extra bottles of chilled water to give away.

Kim makes one positive move a day for someone else.

I'm reading letters the ancestors wrote after arriving

in the land of freedom, words in perfect English script . . .

describing gifts they gave one another for Christmas.

Even the listing seems oddly civilized,

these 1906 Germans . . .*hand-stitched embroideries for dresser*

tops. Bow ties. Slippers, parlor croquet, gold ring, "pretty

inkwell."

How they comforted themselves! A giant roast

made them feel more at home.

Posthumous medals of honor for

coming, continuing—could we do that?

And where would we go?

My father's hope for Palestine

stitching my bones, "no one wakes up and

dreams of fighting around the house"—

someday soon the steady eyes of children in Gaza,

yearning for a little extra electricity

to cool their lemons and cantaloupes, will be known.

Yes?

We talked for two hours via Google Chat,

they did not complain once.   Discussing stories,

books, families, a character who does

what you might do.

Meanwhile secret diplomats are what we must be,

as a girl in Qatar once assured me,

each day slipping its blank visa into our hands.

Communication Skills

I am working on speaking to the ones
who have not spoken to us in years,
the ones swinging punches out of nowhere,
the ones who decided to shun us
for reasons unknown,
who wouldn't greet our group
at the family reunion
but sat across the swimming pool
looking wounded.

The strength of strangers will
help us survive.
Strangers are so generous.
They don't know our faults, our flaws,
so they hope for the best,
muttering good morning
when you pass at the bridge.
The consolation of strangers
is endless and forgiving.

But it takes all our courage

with close ones sometimes.

Families, neighbors, best friends . . .

even if we believe in world peace,

they will find reasons to dislike us.

I think of Gandhi who said

he might never have become

an activist for nonviolence

if the neighbor boys had not

beaten him up.

Exotic Animals, Book for Children

Armadillo means

"little armored one."

Some of us become this to survive

in our own countries.

I would like to see an armadillo

crossing the road.

Our armor is invisible,

it polishes itself.

We might have preferred to be

a softer animal, wouldn't you?

With fur and delicate paws,

like an African Striped Grass Mouse,

also known as Zebra Mouse.

The Frogs Did Not Forget

how to do what they do

through the huge dry days

where were they hiding?

one might lose a tune   abandon a tradition

fall into a crack   but the frogs after the rain

were singing on six notes

outside the bedroom window's

tangle of vines

pleasure poking its throaty resonance

back into my brain

Cross That Line

Paul Robeson stood
on the northern border
of the USA
and sang into Canada
where a vast audience
sat on folding chairs
waiting to hear him.

He sang into Canada.
His voice left the USA
when his body was
not allowed to cross
that line.

Remind us again,
brave friend.
What countries may we
sing into?
What lines should we all

be crossing?

What songs travel toward us

from far away

to deepen our days?

Ted Kooser Is My President

When I travel abroad, I will invoke

Ted's poems at checkpoints:

yes, barns, yes, memory, gentility,

the quiet little wind among stones.

If they ask, *You are American?*

I will say, Ted's kind of American.

No, I carry no scissors or matches.

Yes, horizons, dinner tables.

Yes, weather, the honesty of it.

Buttons, chickens. Feel free

to dump my purse. I'll wander

to the window, stare out for days.

Actually, I have never been

to Nebraska, except with Ted,

who hosted me dozens of times,

though we have never met.

His deep assurance comforts me.

He's not big on torture at all.

He could probably sneak into your country

when you weren't looking

and say something really good about it.

Have you noticed those purple blossoms

in a clump beside your wall?

No One Thinks of Tegucigalpa

No one thinks of Tegucigalpa, unless you are the man
at the Christmas party who sells weapons to Honduras
and smilingly bets on war. Or you have been there,
you wear the miles of markets, a cascading undergarment
beneath your calm white shirt, the slick black tiles
of the plaza, girl coming early, little hum and bucket,
to polish them. Near the river, a toothless man
kept parrots and monkeys in his yard. Por que? He said, "Love."

They don't want to hear about Tegucigalpa because it makes
them feel like a catalogue of omissions. Where is it?
Now who? As if Houston were everything, the sun comes up
because commerce exists . . . but if you kept driving south,
past Mexico's pointed peaks, the grieving villages
of Guatemala, you would reach the city that climbs hills,
opening its pink-lidded eye while the Peace Monument
draws a quiet breath. A boy stands all day skewering peppers
till the night hisses on his grill.

Where is it? At the end of my arm, so close I tap the

red roofs with my finger, the basket seller weaves a

crib for my heart. Think of the countries

you have never seen, the cities of those countries,

start here, then ask, How bad is it to dress

in a cold room? How small your own wish

for a parcel of children? How remarkably invisible

this tear?

Broken

What was precious—flexing.

Fingers wrapping bottle, jar,

fluent weave of tendon, bone and nerve.

To grip a handle, lift the bag of books,

button simply, fold a card—

I did not feel magnificent.

Unthinking movement, come again.

These days of slow re-knitting

stoked with pain . . .

"Revise the scene of injury,"

urged Kathleen, so then I did not

snap against the root, but just became it.

Thank your ankles, thank your wrists,

How many gifts have we not named?

The Rider

A boy told me
if he roller-skated fast enough
his loneliness couldn't catch up to him,
the best reason I ever heard
for trying to be a champion.

What I wonder tonight,
pedaling hard down King William Street,
is if it translates to bicycles.

A victory! To leave your loneliness
panting behind you on some street corner
while you float free into a cloud of sudden azaleas,
luminous pink petals that have never felt loneliness,
no matter how slowly they fell.

Torn Map

Once, by mistake,

she tore a map in half.

She taped it back, but crookedly.

Now all the roads ended in water.

There were mountains

right next to her hometown.

Wouldn't it be nice

if that were true?

I'd tear a map

and be right next to you.

Problems with the Story

The story was too long.

Before you told it, you forgot it.

Before the snake unwound
his infinite body
from around the tree,
the head forgot where he was going.

The story had too many beginnings.

If you stepped through a door,
twelve others might open.

Did anyone have time?

The story, the story, whose was it?

Did someone else own it too?

The story knotted in the throat of a finch.

Sometimes the story felt cold after you told it.

The story might make his mother nervous.

This was only a translation of the story I heard
through a small crack while sleeping.

This was not the best story.

Angels and bells did not follow this story
but still, I had to tell it.

It was the only chance I had
to find you.

Paris

Once my father and I were flying home from the Middle East
and we stopped in Paris for 24 hours.

Our taxi driver told us what happiness was. "It's when you
don't want anything. You don't hate it,

you just don't want it. You like it, in fact. You just don't want it."
I told him he sounded like a Buddhist,

but he didn't want that either. He said nobody in Paris was
happy. He let us off on a street where vendors

sold cream puffs and hosiery and snazzy yellow-toed shoes and
pears and fresh baguettes and wine.

The whole day and night I was in Paris, I bought nothing. Not
one thing. Not even a postcard.

At the restaurant, I asked the waitress to choose for me, partly

because I couldn't read French, but also

because I wasn't sure what I wanted. We could have changed

our tickets and stayed 10 days.

My father wanted to. I could have bought Parisian socks, a tin

of lemon drops. My father kept shaking

his head, asking, "What's the rush?" He told me I'd be sorry

later. It wasn't the first time he'd predicted this.

But I felt happy in Paris, so briefly, breezing up and down those

streets I'd never know with my empty hands.

Gate A-4

Wandering around the Albuquerque Airport Terminal, after
learning my flight had been detained four hours, I heard
an announcement: "If anyone in the vicinity of Gate A-4
understands any Arabic, please come to the gate immediately."
Well—one pauses these days. Gate A-4 was my own gate. I
went there.

An older woman in full traditional Palestinian embroidered
dress, just like my grandma wore, was crumpled to the floor,
wailing. "Help," said the Flight Agent. "Talk to her. What is
her problem? We told her the flight was going to be late, and
she did this." I stooped to put my arm around the woman
and spoke haltingly. *"Shu-dow-a, Shu-bid-uck Habibti? Stani
schway, Min fadlick, Shu-bit-se-wee?"* The minute she heard
any words she knew, however poorly used, she stopped crying.
She thought the flight had been cancelled entirely. She needed
to be in El Paso for major medical treatment the next day. I
said, "You're fine, you'll get there, who's picking you up? Let's

call him." We called her son, I spoke with him in English, saying I would stay with his mother till we got on the plane.

She talked to him. Then we called her other sons just for fun. Then we called my dad and he and she spoke for a while in Arabic and found out of course they had ten shared friends. Then I thought just for the heck of it why not call some Palestinian poets I know and let them chat with her?

This all took up two hours. She was laughing a lot by then. Telling about her life, patting my knee, answering questions. She had pulled a sack of homemade *mamool* cookies—little powdered sugar crumbly mounds stuffed with dates and nuts—from her bag—and was offering them to all the women at the gate. To my amazement, not a single woman declined one. It was like a sacrament. The traveler from Argentina, the mom from California, the lovely woman from Laredo—we were all covered with the same powdered sugar. And smiling. There is no better cookie.

And then the airline broke out free apple juice from huge coolers and two little girls from our flight ran around serving it and they were covered with powdered sugar too. And I noticed my new best friend—by now we were holding hands—had a potted plant poking out of her bag, some medicinal thing, with green furry leaves. Such an old country traveling tradition. Always carry a plant. Always stay rooted to somewhere.

And I looked around that gate of late and weary ones and thought, this is the world I want to live in. The shared world. Not a single person in that gate—once the crying of confusion stopped—seemed apprehensive about any other person. They took the cookies. I wanted to hug all those other women too. This can still happen anywhere. Not everything is lost.

Only Pine Nuts Can Stop a War

The hills were quiet.

Not a single shot was fired.

When local labor is busy with other work

fighting can subside.

The "pine-nut truce"—We will not shoot

for 15 days so the people can collect pine cones.

With the harvest demanding as many hands as possible

fewer men were available to plan attacks.

The men's hands were blackened with dirt and pine sap.

An elder said, *All of our people are involved in pine nuts.*

A medic said, *That was actually very interesting.*

Mediterranean Blue

If you are the child of a refugee, you do not
sleep easily when they are crossing the sea
on small rafts and you know they can't swim.
My father couldn't swim either. He swam through
sorrow, though, and made it to the other side
on a ship, pitching his old clothes overboard
at landing, then tried to be happy, make a new life.
But something inside him was always paddling home,
clinging to anything that floated—a story, a food or face.
They are the bravest people on earth right now,
don't dare look down on them. Each mind a universe
swirling as many details as yours, as much love
for a humble place. Now the shirt is torn,
the sea too wide for comfort, and nowhere
to receive a letter for a very long time.

And if we can reach out a hand, we better.

On Doubt and Bad Reviews

Doubt is easy. You welcome it, your old friend.

Poet Edward Field told a bunch of kids,

Invite it in, feed it a good dinner, give it a place to sleep

on the couch. Don't make it too comfortable or

it might never leave. When it goes away, say okay, I'll see you

again later. Don't fear. Don't give it your notebook.

As for bad reviews, sure. William Stafford advised no credence

to praise or blame. Just steady on.

Once a man named Paul called me "a kid." I liked kids

but I knew he meant it as an insult. Anyway, I *was* a kid.

I guess he was saying, why should we listen to kids?

A newspaper described a woman named Frieda being asked

if "I was serious" and "she whistled." What did that mean?

How do you interpret a whistle? This was one thing

that bothered me.

And where did Frieda ever go?

Common Funeral Myths

1. You need to say goodbye to this person.

2. Each of you is mourning the same individual.

3. The peace which eluded our departed on earth
will now be readily available to him/her/all of us.

4. The conversation is over.

5. Your dreams will vibrate with scenes of this person.

6. The beloved departed wrote you and only you

   a secret farewell note

   which you will find in a couple of years.

World of the future, we thirsted

Stripped of a sense of well-being

we downed our water from small disposable bottles.

Casting the plastic to streetside,

we poured high-potency energy tonics or Coke

down our throats, because this time in history

had sapped us so thoroughly and

we were desperate.

Straws, plastic cups, crushed cans,

in a three-block walk you could fill a sack.

As if we could replenish spirits quickly,

pitching containers without remorse

—who did we imagine would pick them up?

What did we really know of plastic spirals in the sea

bigger than whole countries,

we had never swirled in one ourselves,

as a fish might do, a sea urchin, a whole family of eels,

did we wish to be invincible, using what we wanted,

discarding what we didn't, as in wars,

whole cities and nations crumpled

after our tanks and big guns pull out?

How long does it take to be thirsty again?

We were so lonely in the streets though

all the small houses still had noses, mouths,

eyes from which we might peer, as our fellow-

citizens walk their dogs, pause helplessly as the dogs

circle trees, tip their heads back for a long slow slug

of water or tea, and never fear, never fear.

I Won't Tell

Your signature for entry is an oath of privacy for anything you
experience on Floor 5.

We know how oaths go, these days. He's staring out the streaky
window
at sunset and will not say hello. She's riding the elevator in her
head,
not arriving at Floor 5 where the locked wards are, just being
maybe
a happy person headed for Floor 3. Trust me. We shouldn't be
here.
The tall lady says she never wrote a check in her life, before
Harry died.
That's what sent her here, a checkbook. Wrapped in a huge
black towel,
she says it's the color of oil. Guy with a beard wants to make
people
proud. "Did you know I write songs?" he repeats, to the couch,
and the side-table, and the lamp.

Young lad with a red crewcut earned so much money

he forgot to pay his bills, went wild on a freeway. Money seems

to be a common factor. She had credit card fever.

Could I please bring her some catalogues?

Did you know rehab at Kerrville doesn't always work?

She cut herself with a plastic knife after dinner and wants you

to see. He's stockpiling sugar packets in the fake plant on the

table.

Everyone likes the food and everyone eats something entirely

different

from everyone else. It's against the rules to trade. You had a

menu,

now you're stuck. Isn't that it? You had a menu. We all had a

menu.

On my loved one's first nights here, she wandered into

everyone else's rooms

by mistake, calling people invented names—some they now

prefer

to their own.

Early Bird

wishes you well

picks a few high notes

and believes in them

matching riffs with

invisible twin

next tree

impossible to be gloomy

under such clear tones

priming light

sticks sticks

someone needs sticks

make your nest pretty

Early doesn't know

what humans do

doesn't need to

Lake Oswego

In the hotel lobby,

a tall man wearing a clanky tool belt

is asking for the boiler in the basement

before 8 a.m. It's raining, been raining for days.

So foggy and cold, I slept in my winter coat

inside my room.

The man wears boots, dark work clothes,

casting me back so hard

like that sucking sound a phone makes

sending a message, I'm being messaged

by the past, the dignity of a worker

who shows up on time,

Daddy's grave face

as he rises from table to greet him,

welcome *My Friend*.

The broken washer, the stove,

a mysterious man smelling of oil,

but a quiet rush of confidence

lifting the room—

He knows how to fix it.

Window

Hope makes itself every day

springs up from the tiniest places

No one gives it to us

we just notice it

quiet in the small moment

The 2-year-old

"kissing the window" he said

because someone he loved

was out there

Long Marriage

We share a napkin

You use the inside

I'll use the outside

    he says

Confluence

Lost Spanish homework

snagged on a crocus

nada—nadie—nunca

same day they memorialized you

Do Not Touch the Puffins

I admit I wanted to.

They were so enthusiastic,

waddle of black and white,

their orange feet.

You were still young then,

we sat on a pile of stones,

Isle of Staffa,

whispering people who'd hiked up

from the boat.

You liked the idea of an island

only for birds.

The puffins nuzzled our shoes

curiously,

hey, they're touching us,

wondering what we were,

such big things

with our mitts

poked into our jeans.

Grocery Store

There was more to be made, always.

Something to try that you might like.

And the lines of spices packed with their little fragrant faith . . .

my friend wrote, years ago, before so many more people died,

"Let me know how your trees grow, flower, and fruit."

What was she referring to? The stunted lemon

that never made a lemon but proclaimed its presence

with staggering thorns? The leaning apricot

not even the birds liked to sit in?

I could tally mistakes easier than triumphs

which felt like a good thing, somehow,

a rod to stand tall by, tying back the pink roses

drooping their faces to the ground.

We had cried in the checkout line,

recognizing one another after all these years.

No way, she said, *you saved me.*

Not true, I said, *it was all you.*

And the cashier with her hand full of coins

tipped her head patiently—

the next person's cart was even fuller.

Montana Before Breakfast

It's right down that road, she said,

pointing a spoon—*you could get there and*

back before the coffee's gone.

Yellow butterflies circled high

above dirt road. Some rancher

had posted a mean Obama sign.

How could you live

in wide grassland glory

and be rude?

I crossed a cattle guard,

said hey to the cattle,

took one picture of my last state

yet to see

and turned around.

I couldn't wait to get back to Wyoming.

Mona's Taco

Dear Mona, do you know

how your old building's smooth stucco lines

mark the spot of Something True?

The hand-lettered sign rises up,

a flag on Highway 90 West.

Surely familiar combinations

reign inside,

bean & cheese, potato & egg,

perhaps a specialty of your own making—

avocado twist or smoky salsa.

Where are you, Mona, when the moon rises

over Castroville? Your sign says CLOSED.

The singularity of your *nombre* touches me.

One taco might be enough.

Here come the ranchers who just lived through

the worst drought and flood back-to-back

and the truckers on the Del Rio route,

hats with an oily brim.

Don't we all need someone to greet us

to make us feel we're here?

West of town, soft fields

ease our city-cluttered eyes.

There's a rim of hills to hope for up ahead.

Mona, mysterious Mona,

I think I love you.

Every morning I muse, *Mona's up.*

Tanya's Winter

1

A body leaves the world.
But do its hopes leave the world?

No one can see you anymore.
But here, two purple flowers blooming side by side,
in the chill.

Amon recalls that sitting in a coffee shop with you
and your friends felt like the old country.
Everywhere you were was the old country.

This could keep someone going. Here we make a table.
Six inches square.

On earth, the door still swings wide open.
We live in a new thought.

2

Rivers promise wherever we move will be somewhere,
maybe a root to hold on to,

and always, so many suffer more than we do.

Can you feel a current inside?

Don't try to explain.

3

Tanya said the Russian winter will never leave her,

avenues of snow between massive buildings, black trees.

The depth of it, like silences she would give her life to.

Big Song

Under the bridge at Washington Street

    a man with acoustic guitar

  was plucking and singing again   in Spanish

    always only in Spanish

  once I would have called him an old man

before I got old   now no one is old

  his voice amplifying   thanks to the bridge

shivering off iron girders   echoing concrete walls

becoming so huge   as if through a megaphone

but sweeter   rich and round   giant sugar cookie

  of a voice traveling to our side of the river

   my three-year-old walking partner

twirled in place   *that sounds big*

never asking   *why would a man be singing?*

near our chattering ducks

who never lose hope we might one day

defy the signs and *feed them*

river reeds   blooming yellow bells of Esperanza

only a few hours distance   from camps of wire and concrete

thin mattresses   aluminum foil sheets

sisters and brothers whose stories we can't really know

whatever we think about them   what happens next

how hard it has been

who is this man?   so many years

singing in winter   summer   no cup beside him

not asking for anything　　people run past with their dogs

ears plugged　　their own music

I don't know where he lives

secret stories under the bridge

all these years of echo

boy raising his arms

dipping and stepping

singer　　nodding his head

glad to be heard

raising one hand　　to both of us twirling

　　—solamente　por que?
　　—siempre　por que?

Altar of the Steaming Cup

I'm not asking you to solve it, he said.
I'm just moving it out of my mind.

She spooned honey into her mint tea as if
a sacrament in the stirring.

Some people saw snow on the pass.
Some people saw foxes and deer.
Three saw coiled snakes
near the abandoned porcelain bathtub.

Rhubarb cobbler—and we ate it all.

Everyone adjusting—here, take my extra comforter,
give this plush vest to your mom, she'll need it.

Take these extra notebooks.

Finding space, arranging space.

In the presence of places that don't belong to me

I feel most free.

Something yellow on the desk.

No deep thoughts in the dark, Edith said.

And she lived to be 100.

Getting Older, Japan

Salt in the sea,

you befriend me.

I'm washing up

on the shores of something.

Whether or not

I want to be here

is no longer relevant.

The red train flies by

outside my window

every six minutes or so.

I feel immense tenderness

for the people getting on it.

His Love

Gene Wesley Elder

leaving his life

wrapping household goods

kitchen cups

spoons

tiny tablecloths

grandma's china plates

in rumpled wrapping paper

snagged with ribbons

brown grocery bags

distributed to friends

ordering no memorials

give your money to an artist

who needs it

give my money to artists

just call my lawyer

get the money

take time

arrange things under trees

sit with them

make constellations of

cast-offs

till beauty rises

no I'm not scared

I'm just doing what we all do

sooner or later

lucky I had time to savor

think about what I lived

parcel things out

I wanted the windows and doors

left open

long last days

quiet filters

a few opera songs

deleted my emails

after writing a final one

THE END IS NEAR

ARTIST GOING UNDERGROUND

remember me   but even more

remember you

Blue River of Florida Light

To fall into a day.

Wide horizon every day of a life.

Nothing stops moving or changing, ever.

Sea swallows all our mutterings.

Who did you hope to meet?

What were you looking for?

Some dreams had tight hems, but not here.

You couldn't tell which way the laughter was blowing.

Kindness

Before you know what kindness really is

you must lose things

feel the future dissolve in a moment

like salt in a weakened broth.

What you held in your hand,

what you counted and carefully saved,

this must go so you know

how desolate the landscape can be

between the regions of kindness.

How you ride and ride

thinking the bus will never stop,

the passengers eating maize

will stare out the window forever.

Before you learn the tender gravity of kindness,

you must travel where the Indian in a white poncho

lies dead by the side of the road.

You must see how this could be you,

he too was someone

who journeyed through the night with plans

and the simple breath that kept him alive.

Before you know kindness as the deepest thing inside,

you must know sorrow as the other deepest thing.

You must wake up with sorrow.

You must speak to it till your voice

catches the thread of all sorrows

and you see the size of the cloth.

Then it is only kindness that makes sense anymore,

only kindness that ties your shoes

and sends you out into the day to gaze at bread,

only kindness that raises its head

from the crowd of the world to say,

It is I you have been looking for,

and then goes with you everywhere

like a shadow or a friend.

Slim Thoughts

Two helpful words to keep in mind at the beginning of any writing adventure are pleasure and spaciousness. If we connect a sense of joy with our writing, we may be inclined to explore further. What's there to find out? Perhaps too much stock has been placed in big ideas or even small ones—a myth!—but regularity seems like a key. Don't start with a big idea. Start with a phrase, a line, a quote. Questions are very helpful. Begin with a few you're carrying right now. Starting with friction can be useful. The Texas writer William Goyen used to say, "I always start with trouble."

Small increments of writing time may matter more than we could guess. One thing leads to many—swerving off, linking up, opening of voices and images and memories. Nearby notebooks—or iPads or tablets or laptops—are surely helpful. I still favor the pencil and pen on the page, the tactile joy of it (as a child I was thrilled to have fallen in love with the "cheapest art") because I still love the visible arrangement of lines made by hand, and the very slight brushy pencil sound.

Whatever your preferred method, make a plan, and return to it. It's a party to which we keep inviting ourselves.

And we all have so many realms of material that are very close by:

Families

Neighborhoods

Changes

Memories

Spoken language woven into poems—something someone said to you a long time ago and you still remember it—why, out of all the talk, do you remember that thing?

Pets

Losses

First Times

Last Times

Fears

Friends

Being Sick, Being Well

What we see out our windows

Gifts

History—what used to be in this very place where we are sitting now?

Start anywhere.

Spaciousness—any page is wider than it looks. You have no idea where this thing might be going. Write in nuggets—here are my questions, here are some details I saw within the last 24 hours, here are some quotes I heard people say today. Gather material first—then select and connect from it.

Give up the annoying question, "How long does this have to be?" Just wonder—how long does it *need* to be? Then try to find out.

Each thing gives us something else.

The more any of us writes, the more our words will "come to us." If we trust in the words and their own mysterious relationships with one another, they will help us find things out. Thinking as we write is as much a skill as thinking in advance and planning it all, possibly a tactic more helpful for book reports or science projects than for poetry.

Consider the pleasure we feel when we go to a beach. The broad breath, the bigger air, the endless swish of movement and backdrop of sound.

We feel uplifted, exhilarated. Writing regularly can help us feel that way too. It slows and eases us, calms us down. Having a focal point is generative. Consider the spaciousness of the sky over the water, which we often forget about as we scurry through our days. I love what the poet Marvin Bell has suggested about writing—*Read something, then write something. Read something else, then write something else.* It's all connected, it's always been connected. Let one activity inform the other. Streams of language exchanging their powers.

I do believe in overwriting, then cutting back. Physical fitness of the pen, page, and mind, interwoven. If you believe in revision you don't have to worry about perfection. Try not to worry about anything. It's impossible, of course, but try. I do think writing will help you live your life.

Notes on Poems

"Yellow Glove" took place in Ferguson, Missouri, the neighborhood of Greater St. Louis where I grew up from ages 2–13. Ferguson was unobtrusive, historic, filled with old houses and giant trees, and had once been a giant farmland. No one would ever have guessed the quiet town would later be the scene of racial violence and public demonstrations, birthplace of the important movement BLACK LIVES MATTER, or that the name "Ferguson" would become widely known. The mysteries of segregation and "lines made by adults" did confound us in the 1950s and early 1960s, and we asked a lot of questions.

"It is not a game, it was never a game" was written after a photograph by Alan Pogue, of Austin, of a young girl in Iraq who lost her precious arm because of war.

"Everything in our world did not seem to fit" is for Palestine—the many generations of refugees, displaced and occupied people, since 1948 and ongoing.

"Wedding Cake" was written after a flight from London to

Riyadh, Saudi Arabia, on British Airways. The mother's attire had changed so dramatically by the time of her return to pick up her baby (and yes, she appeared to have washed her hair in the tiny airliner sink as a few strands were poking out wet from her loose black hijab) that I truly did not recognize her.

"Window" was written for Connie Lowe at the annual spontaneous "Poetry for the People" event founded by the late Kathleen Sommers, San Antonio.

"Grocery Store" is for Charles Butt.

"Confluence" is for Peter Matthiessen, as is "Lying While Birding" and I do think it important to note, in these times, that lying is usually not a good idea.

"Only Pine Nuts Can Stop a War" is a found poem, consisting of actual lines rearranged from a *New York Times* story, Oct. 7, 2011. I only added the title.

"Common Funeral Myths" was a real title of a brochure I found on the ground while collecting trash. I just wrote my own.

"Editorial Suggestions" is a found poem. Every line referred to one draft or another of *The Turtle of Oman*, when the book was still in process.

Gene Wesley Elder was a college classmate, a joyous artist, and an important activist for LGBTQ rights in San Antonio, Texas, even in the earlier days when such public work was rare. He founded the "HAPPY Archives."

Acknowledgments

Deepest gratitude to my brilliant editor Virginia Duncan, who has believed in my work for 30 years. Thanks to Lois Adams, Paul Zakris, everyone at Greenwillow Books; Eliza Fischer, who has graciously organized my travels for years, and Steven Barclay. For all dear friends and family, especially Michael Nye and Miriam Shihab, Madison and Tess, Carol, Kelly, Marky, and my personal guru, Connor James. For all the schools that have granted me harbor over the many years. For teachers, especially Lisa Siemens of Manitoba, Lucy McCormick Calkins, and in memory of Dr. John David Brantley—it was an honor to be your assistant forever and ever. For the great tribe of poets and friends of poetry in every country. For visual artists, especially Paula Owen and in memory of Katie Pell. For photographers, especially Alexei Wood and the Langmore family. For J. D. Linton, where are you now? For Marie Brenner and Marion Winik! For all the traders, missed so much during pandemic time. For Ryushin Paul Haller. For all the medical professionals, who work so hard and selflessly every day. Thank you, Rafael López, for your most gorgeous art.

Gratitude to the *New Yorker* ("World of the future, we thirsted"); the *New York Times*; the *Texas Observer*; the Academy of American Poets (Poets.org); *Cordite Review* (Australia); *The Best American Poetry 2019*, edited by Major Jackson (Scribner Poetry, an imprint of Simon & Schuster, 2019), in which "You Are Your Own State Department" appeared; Greenwillow Books, HarperCollins Publishers; the University of South Carolina Press; and State Street Press. Thanks again to U2 for taking "United" and "Kindness" on tour with them.

Index of First Lines

Just last week, nearly three years since you flew, 154

light up our backyard, 13
Lost Spanish homework, 204
Lyda Rose asked, "Are you a grown-up?" 161

Music lives inside my legs, 59
My brother, in his small white bed, 17
My grandparents sold, 148
My Jewish friends are kind and gentle, 74

No one thinks of Tegucigalpa, unless you are the man, 179
Not for him and his people alone, 102

Once, by mistake, 183
Once my father and I were flying home from the Middle East, 186
Once on a plane, 115
Once they started invading us, taking our houses, 89
One by one, 127
One night my grandmother and I, 43
On the first day of his life, 63
Our voices poured out through, 28
Overnight, & quietly. Beneath the scratchy, 38

Paul Robeson stood, 175
Possibly I began writing as a refuge from our insulting first, 14

Salt in the sea, 218
scurried around a classroom papered with poems, 140
Seagulls startle, soar, 58